ALWAYS IN TROUBLE

For Austin —C.D.

For Eli —N.Z.J.

This book was originally published by Scholastic Press in 2009.

ISBN-13: 978-0-545-20413-2
ISBN-10: 0-545-20413-5

12 11 10 9 8 7 6 5 4 3 2   9 10 11 12 13 14/0

Printed in China

This edition first printing, September 2009

The text type was set in Jacoby Light. The display type was set in Eatwell Chubby.

Book design by Pamela Notarantonio

ALWAYS IN TROUBLE

SCHOLASTIC INC.
New York Toronto London Auckland
Sydney Mexico City New Delhi Hong Kong

 Written by Corinne Demas & Pictures by Noah Z. Jones

Emma's dog, Toby, was always in trouble.

On Monday he got into the garbage.

On Tuesday he ran into the road.

On Wednesday he ate a loaf of bread that Emma's dad had just baked.

On Thursday he barked in the middle of the night.

On Friday he wet the rug.

On Saturday he chewed up all the buttons on Emma's new coat.

On Sunday he snoozed.

But on Monday morning he got into the garbage again.

"Something has to be done about that dog!"
said Emma's mom.

"Maybe he isn't getting
enough attention," said Emma.

So all day Monday she gave Toby lots of attention.

She took him for walks

and brushed his fur

and sang him silly songs.

But on Tuesday Toby ate a box of crayons.

On Wednesday he jumped into the basket of clean laundry that Emma's mom had just finished folding.

He was very good on Thursday.

He was very good on Friday.

But on Saturday he chewed up a magazine.

And on Sunday he went wading in the muddy brook and then ran across the clean kitchen floor.

"Something has to be done about that dog!"
cried Emma's mom.

"Maybe he needs to go to dog training school," said Emma.

"What a great idea!" said Emma's mom.

The first class started the next day.

There were ten dogs in Toby's class.

Some were big and some were little. Some barked
and some yipped and some growled and some whined.

Toby was quiet as a goldfish.

He behaved perfectly at school every week,
and he did everything just right.

When Emma said "Sit!"
he sat.

When Emma said "Come!"
he came.

When Emma said "Heel!"
he stood right by her side.

"He was the best dog," said Ms. Katz, the teacher, when the classes were all over. At graduation she gave Toby a diploma with a gold seal.

Emma's mom tacked the diploma low down on the wall, right over Toby's dog dish. "Now you know how to behave," she said to Toby.

But on Monday Toby got into the garbage.

On Tuesday he ran into the road.

On Wednesday he ate the cookies that Emma's dad had just baked.

On Thursday he barked in the middle of the night and woke everyone up.

On Friday he wet the rug.

On Saturday he dug up the petunias Emma and her mom had just planted.

On Sunday he chewed up his diploma.

"Something has to be done about that dog!"
cried Emma's mom.

Emma took him back to dog school.

"Does he sit?"
asked Ms. Katz.

"Yes," said Emma.

"Does he come?"
asked Ms. Katz.

"Yes," said Emma.

"Does he heel?"
asked Ms. Katz.

"Yes," said Emma.

"Well then, what's
the trouble?"
asked Ms. Katz.

So Emma told her.

"I see," said Ms. Katz. "If you want a specially trained dog, you'll have to leave him with me for the week."

"OK," said Emma.

Emma missed Toby all week. He was very happy to see her when she picked him up.

"I hope you've learned something this time,"
said Emma's mom.

"Please, Toby," Emma whispered to him,
"you've got to be good now."

Toby licked Emma's face. He had a strange
twinkle in his eye.

On Monday he took out the garbage.

On Tuesday he baked some bread.

On Wednesday he vacuumed the rug.

On Thursday he folded the laundry.

On Friday he washed the kitchen floor.

On Saturday he planted some petunias.

And on Sunday he snoozed.

But no dog can be perfect always — not even Toby.